KU-438-706

Copyright © 1986 Hasbro Inc and The Walt Disney Company.
All rights reserved.
Published in Great Britain by World International Publishing Limited.
An Egmont Company,
Egmont House, P.O. Box 111, Great Ducie Street, Manchester M60 3BL.
Printed in Belgium. SBN 7235 7173 2.

Wuzzles

THE WUZZLES™ AND THE HAUNTED CASTLE

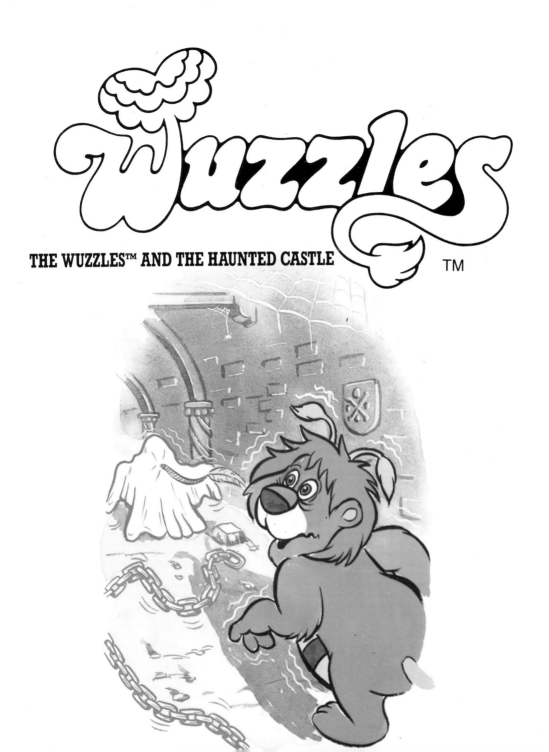

The Wuzzles and the Haunted Castle

Bumblelion was just rowing around the lake for the hundredth time when he saw Moosel sitting under a tree. Sitting under a tree doing nothing. Well, he was doing something; he was holding a fishing rod in one hand and a toasted cucumelon in the other, and he was listening to the radio. But to Bumblelion that was doing nothing.

Bumblelion looked up as

he heard someone shouting to him. "Hey, Bumblelion, do you like my new flying picnic basket?" Rhinokey laughed as he looked down from his hot air balloon. "I've got lots of food here. I'm staying up all day."

As he rowed harder and harder, Bumblelion muttered crossly to himself, "Wailing Wuzzles! There's too much nothing going on. Moosel's just sitting under a tree, Rhinokey's up in the sky just sitting in a flying picnic basket, and when I went past Butterbear's she was just sitting in her garden talking to Hoppo and Eleroo. I'll have to do something about all this."

It was an hour later, while he was having a cold shower, that Bumblelion nearly thought of something. A picture flashed into his head. A picture of a house. No, it wasn't a house it was a . . . "What was it?" muttered Bumblelion.

"What did I nearly remember? It's no good, I'll have to go for a bike ride, that always helps me to think." Bumblelion dried himself quickly with his towel worker, and picking up his sunhat, he hurried out to his garden.

in her garden with Hoppo and Eleroo when Bumblelion rode past. "I wonder where he's going?" she said. "He's got a lot of food with him – and a bunch of flowers."

"I might be going a long way," said Bumblelion to himself, as he wheeled his barrowbike out of the shed. "I'll take something to eat and I'd better take some flowers as well." Bumblelion picked some applenuts, a ripe plumelon, a big carroturnip and a large bunch of flowers. Soon he was ready to go.

Butterbear was still sitting

"Oh no," groaned Hoppo. "When Bumblelion rides his bike, he's usually planning something. And if he's got flowers with him that's even worse. You know how he needs to smell flowers when he's thinking. Well I don't want to do anything except lie here and sunbathe so I hope he isn't planning anything for us." Hoppo rolled over onto her back. "I wish I had my suntan cream with me. I don't want to get wrinkled skin."

"I've got some in my pouch. I'll find it for you, Hoppo," said Eleroo shyly. He was very fond of Hoppo and was pleased to think that there was something he could do for her.

"Eleroo, what a load of

junk!" laughed Butterbear, as her friend pulled all sorts of things out of his pouch to find the suntan cream. "What's this for?"

"It's a backwhistle," said Eleroo. "And this isn't junk. It will all come in handy one day, I know it will. Ah, here's the cream, Hoppo."

Eleroo took the lid off the jar of cream and was just about to pass it to Hoppo when Butterbear blew the backwhistle. There was a loud screeching noise and at the same moment, a long tube with a feather on the end, shot out and tickled Eleroo's back!

11

on your face anyway," laughed Butterbear, looking at Hoppo. "There's no room for anything else with all that cream over it."

"Scrape some cream off her face and put it on the rest of her," said Eleroo. "Look, you can use this scraper."

"Eleroo!" gurgled Hoppo. "You've poured the cream all over my face and it's gone in my mouth, too. Ugh, it tastes horrible."

"I'm sorry Hoppo," stammered Eleroo. "The backwhistle made me jump."

"You won't get wrinkles

At last, the three Wuzzles were sunbathing peacefully again. Hoppo and Eleroo were asleep, and Butterbear was almost asleep, when there was a strange hissing noise from just above them. Opening a sleepy eye, Butterbear glanced up. She stared in dismay, then yelled out a warning, but she was too late. Rhinokey and his flying picnic basket zoomed down to the ground right on top of Hoppo and Eleroo!

"Whimpering Wuzzles!" shrieked Rhinokey. "My hot air balloon burst. Oh, my picnic basket, my beautiful picnic basket!"

Rhinokey pulled in vain at the picnic basket. From underneath it came the sound of Hoppo and Eleroo struggling to get free.

"My front tooth is broken, I'm sure it is," howled Hoppo. "Oh, I'm going to look such a mess. Get me out of here. Eleroo, do something."

Eleroo would have loved to do something to get Hoppo and himself from under the basket but his trunk, which had been squashed into one of Butterbear's flowerbeds, was full of soil and he was trying not to choke.

"Look at my flowers, they're all getting so squashed," wailed Butterbear. "Get your basket off them, Rhinokey."

"Don't stand there wailing. Help me pull," shouted Rhinokey. "My tea is under there. That's getting squashed, too!"

Hoppo was getting angrier and angrier. She pushed and kicked with all her might and suddenly the basket flew off, knocking Rhinokey and Butterbear over. "A mirror, get me a mirror," she shouted. "I must look at my tooth. Get up, Eleroo, and look in your pouch. You must have a mirror there somewhere."

Hoppo heaved Eleroo to his feet and as she did so, Eleroo choked, splattering soil all over her. "Oh, you're all so clumsy!" shouted Hoppo. "I'm not staying here another second. I'm going home."

"I'm sorry, Hoppo," called Eleroo, who had stopped choking. "I couldn't help it, I . . ." But Hoppo had gone.

15

"Leave her alone and help me with my flowers," said Butterbear, scrambling to her feet. "Oh the poor, poor things. Just look at them."

"I'm sorry. I couldn't help it," said Eleroo once again.

"I wish you'd stop saying you're sorry," said Rhinokey, jumping up. "It's all my fault this happened, not yours, Eleroo. Why do you have to take the blame for everything?" Poor Eleroo felt so upset that he went home, too.

"You can take your basket and go as well," said Butterbear. "I want to be alone with my poor squashed flowers."

"I'll go and see if Moosel can fix it," sighed Rhinokey, looking at his bent basket. "Just look at it."

Butterbear didn't take any notice, she was too busy crooning to her flowers, so Rhinokey picked up his basket and went to find Moosel.

Meanwhile, Bumblelion had found what he'd been trying to think of. He'd ridden for quite a few miles, right round the far side of the lake and into a lonely hilly area. And there it was right on top of the highest hill. "The tumbledown castle!" said Bumblelion.

17

"Waltzing Wuzzles, I must stop and smell some flowers. Then I'll be able to work out a really good plan."

Early next morning, Bumblelion rang the Wuzzle buzzerbell to call a meeting in the village hall. One by one, the other Wuzzles arrived. "I was giving myself a face pack," grumbled Hoppo. "I'm sure I got some freckles yesterday when we were sunbathing."

"It was hot," said Rhinokey. "I think my hot air balloon burst because it got too hot."

"Yes, and my tooth has got a crack in it from your

flying picnic basket," said Hoppo. "Why did you have to land on us?"

Moosel and Butterbear were arguing when they arrived. "We were racing paper boats," explained Butterbear. "Mine was just about to win when the buzzerbell rang."

"Mine would have won, not yours," said Moosel. "Yours was just about to get stuck behind that log."

"No it was . . ." began Butterbear, but Bumblelion had jumped onto the platform and was banging the gong for silence.

19

"Where's Eleroo?" he shouted. "I want all of you to hear my plan."

Just then Eleroo hurried in. "I'm sorry I took so long," he said. "I got stuck in my hammock. I had to tear a big hole in it before I could get out. I'll have to bring it to your fix-it shop, Moosel."

"Oh, I've closed my shop for a while," said Moosel. "It's too hot to work."

"Will you all be quiet and listen?" roared Bumblelion. "You're all just spending the days doing nothing at all. Well, it's got to stop. As from tomorrow we're going to rebuild the tumbledown castle. I went to look at it yesterday. All the stones are there and I've got plenty of cement we can take with us."

"But it's miles and miles away to the old castle," said Hoppo. "How are we going to get there?"

"It's much too hot to start building things," groaned Moosel.

"My plants need a lot of water in this hot weather," explained Butterbear. "I can't spend hours and hours every day away from home."

"My collections need sorting out," said Eleroo. "I've got lots to do."

Rhinokey was the only one who didn't have anything to say. He didn't want to spend the hot

summer days building up the old castle but . . . . He chuckled silently to himself. "I can use some of the things that Eleroo left behind yesterday," he whispered. "Just think. If my hot air balloon hadn't burst, my basket wouldn't have landed on top of Eleroo and I wouldn't have found all those bits and pieces from Eleroo's pouch."

"Oh well," shouted Bumblelion. "I suppose I'll have to rebuild the castle by myself. It's a shame that none of you are strong enough or clever enough to help me."

That did it of course. All the Wuzzles thought they were strong and clever. They'd show Bumblelion! So it was decided. The Wuzzles would leave early the next morning in the airbus and begin to rebuild the tumbledown castle.

Once Bumblelion had disappeared to sort out his cement, the others started to grumble again. "We had to agree to it," sighed Hoppo. "We are strong and clever . . ."

"But we just want to laze around in the sun," laughed Rhinokey. "And we still can."

"How?" asked Moosel. "You know what Bumblelion's like. He'll want us to work, work, work."

"Leave it to me," grinned Rhinokey. "If I'm not here in the morning when you're ready to leave, just tell Bumblelion that I've gone on ahead."

Rhinokey wasn't there in the morning and Bumblelion was really pleased to hear that he'd gone on ahead. Rhinokey must be keen to start building, he thought to himself. Poor Bumblelion, what a shock he was going to get!

Meanwhile, Rhinokey had been very busy inside the old castle. "You're sure you know what to do?" he asked Koalakeet.

"Of course I'm sure," replied Koalakeet. "I've worked out exactly where to stand. You see, the dial on my wind machine is pointing this way, which means the wind is coming in from that direction. Consequently, if I stand here and you cover me with the sheet . . ."

"All right, I believe you," said Rhinokey, who could never quite understand the words Koalakeet used.

"Now, Piggypine. You do know what you've got to say when they arrive, don't you?"

"I might not use long words," bristled Piggypine, "but I'm not stupid. I know exactly what to say."

"Get ready to say it then. I can hear the airbus

coming," said Koalakeet. "Quickly, Rhinokey. Cover me up and make haste to your own position."

"He means hurry up with everything," laughed Piggypine, who was quite used to Koalakeet's way of speaking.

Rhinokey carefully

covered Koalakeet. "You have got the backwhistle haven't you?" he whispered. "All right, you don't have to blow it. Not yet anyway." And Rhinokey giggled as he climbed onto a rafter just above Koalakeet.

Piggypine had hurried outside and was jumping up and down when the airbus drove up. "Oh Bumblelion, I *am* glad you're here," she called. "Rhinokey asked me to come and help him start

work on the castle, and . . ." Piggypine gulped and buried her head in her trotters. "And every time we picked up a lump of stone there was this terrible noise and something kept brushing our faces. Then, Rhinokey was fixing a rafter and this g-g-ghost appeared. It's still there and Rhinokey can't get down."

Bumblelion turned pale. If there was one thing he was frightened of it was ghosts! However, he didn't want the other Wuzzles to know that, so calling to them to follow him, he strode into the castle. He could hear Rhinokey moaning to himself and he hurried over to talk to him. Before Bumblelion could say a word, there was a terrible

screeching noise, something tickled his face and something else white and scary swayed around in front of him. Then a length of chain, making strange

clanking noises, wriggled across the floor towards Bumblelion!

Bumblelion ran howling out of the castle, banging into the others who were on their way in. "The castle is haunted!" he howled. "We can't work here. Someone go and get Rhinokey."

"I'll go," said Moosel bravely. He'd guessed that Rhinokey had planned the haunting.

"We'll help you," said Butterbear, Eleroo and Hoppo, trying not to giggle.

And while Bumblelion sat moaning to himself in the airbus, Rhinokey showed his friends how he'd turned the castle into a haunted castle.

"Koalakeet hid under this

sheet and blew Eleroo's backwhistle," he giggled. "Piggypine crept in behind Bumblelion and used a walking stick to wriggle the chain across the floor."

"All these things are parts of my collections," said Eleroo. "Where did you find them, Rhinokey?"

"I know," laughed Butterbear. "You must have left them in my garden that day Rhinokey fell out of the sky. You said they'd come in handy one day, Eleroo. Remember?"

Just then, Bumblelion tooted the hornbell. Soon, the Wuzzles were on their way home. "Back to lying in the sun, back to doing nothing," they whispered gleefully. Yes, even Bumblelion was looking forward to it. At least until he'd recovered from the shock of the haunted castle!